WE WAS ROBBED

David Orme lives in Winchester and is the author of a wide range of poetry books, textbooks and picture books for children. When he is not writing he visits schools, performing poetry, running workshops and encouraging children and teachers to enjoy poetry.

Marc S. Vyvyan-Jones' footballing skills are rivalled only by those of his two cats, Mr Claude and Mrs Finknottle, who beat him regularly. He's much better at drawing and has illustrated dozens of books for children. (The cats' drawing is rubbish!) He lives and works with his wife Lucy, a writer, in a cottage near the sea, in Somerset.

Also by David Orme

'ERE WE GO!
Football Poems

YOU'LL NEVER WALK ALONE
More Football Poems

DRACULA'S AUNTIE RUTHLESS
and other Petrifying Poems

SNOGGERS
Slap 'n' Tickle Poems

NOTHING TASTES QUITE LIKE A GERBIL
and other Vile Verses

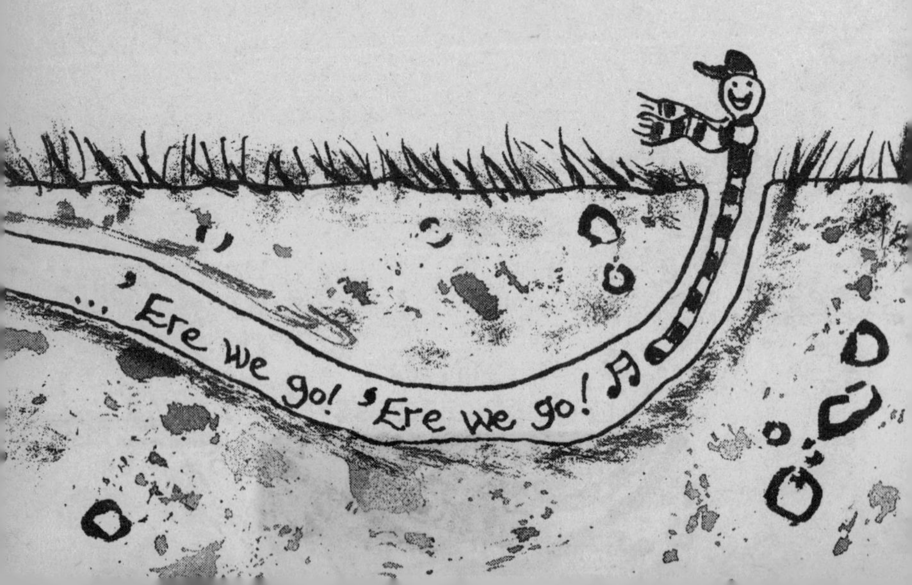

WE WAS ROBBED

YET MORE FOOTBALL POEMS

chosen by DAVID ORME

and illustrated by

Marc Vyvyan-Jones

MACMILLAN
CHILDREN'S BOOKS

First published 1997 by
Macmillan Children's Books
a division of Macmillan Publishers Ltd
25 Eccleston Place London SW1W 9NF
and Basingstoke

Associated companies throughout the world

ISBN 0 330 35005 6

1 3 5 7 9 8 6 4 2

A CIP catalogue record for this book is available from the British Library.

Typeset by Macmillan Children's Books
Printed by Mackays of Chatham Plc, Kent

...walk alone!

CONTENTS

Football Facts

More Worms at Wembley

'Watch out!' cried the first worm
as the centre tried to shoot.
'You only just missed me
with your great big boot.'

'Yes, careful,' said the second,
'With your clumsy great hoof.
Just remember: you're running
about on our roof.'

Then the ball hit the net
and the crowd roared, 'GOAL!'
So the third worm simply sighed
and retreated down its hole.

Tony Mitton

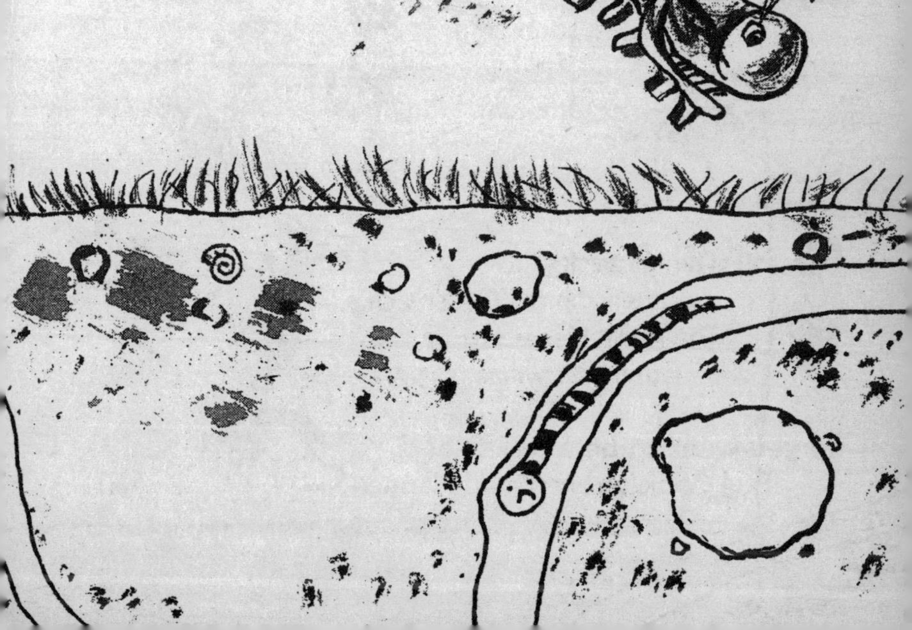

A Football Amulet

From the fans' throats
 the raucous roar,
The raucous roar
 then the goalkeeper's throw,

The goalkeeper's throw
 then the sweeper's pass,
The sweeper's pass
 then the full back's flick,

The full back's flick
 then the midfielder's chip,
The midfielder's chip
 then the winger's run,

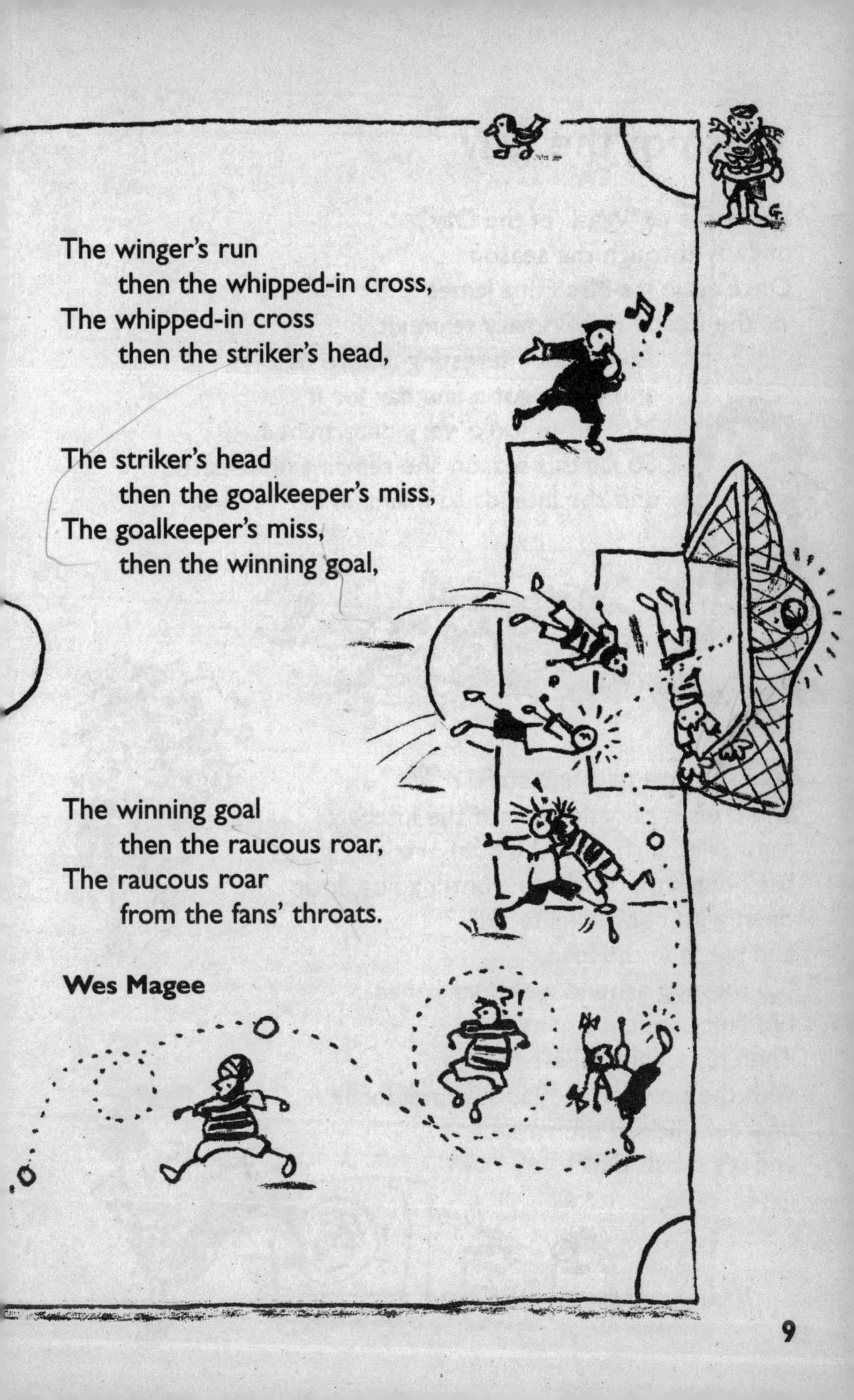

The winger's run
    then the whipped-in cross,
The whipped-in cross
    then the striker's head,

The striker's head
    then the goalkeeper's miss,
The goalkeeper's miss,
    then the winning goal,

The winning goal
    then the raucous roar,
The raucous roar
    from the fans' throats.

Wes Magee

Wash of the Day

Welcome to 'Wash of the Day',
midway through the season.
Once again it's Mrs Edna James
vs. the Castle Hill Primary team kit.
Always an interesting fixture this
and we've got a fine day for it.
Mrs James looks very determined.
So far this season she remains undefeated
and she intends to maintain her record.

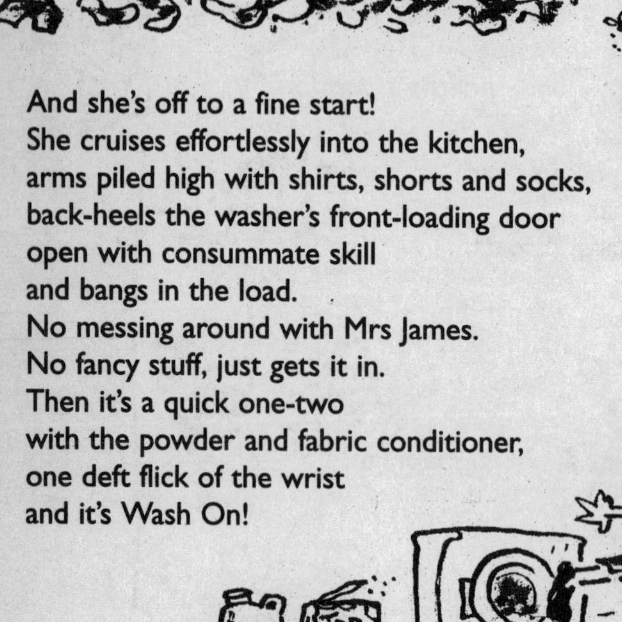

And she's off to a fine start!
She cruises effortlessly into the kitchen,
arms piled high with shirts, shorts and socks,
back-heels the washer's front-loading door
open with consummate skill
and bangs in the load.
No messing around with Mrs James.
No fancy stuff, just gets it in.
Then it's a quick one-two
with the powder and fabric conditioner,
one deft flick of the wrist
and it's Wash On!

The action's non-stop.
The kit soaks up the punishment.
But it's no contest.
Wash.
Rinse.
Spin dry
and then a quick transfer
to a laundry basket
and it's out into the back garden.

There's no stopping Mrs James now!
Pace, stamina, vision – she's got
the lot.
She's poetry in motion.
Before you can say 'non-bio'
she's got everything pegged-up.
What a line-up!
And it's all as clean as a whistle.
It's all over bar the shouting.
A sparkling performance!

What can you say about this woman?
She's sensational.
In a league of her own.

(To the tune of 'You'll Never Walk Alone':)

'Waaassh on! Waaassh on!
With soap from the start –
And you'll never wa-ash alone
You'll never waaassh a-lone!'

Tony Langham

Every Game's a Home Game with my Footy Family

Grandad's in the goal
Dad's in defence
Mother's in midfield
Baby's on the bench

Sister's centre forward
Brother's at the back
Cousin is the coach
Auntie's in attack

Nana is the manager
and just because I missed
a penalty last home match
I'm on the transfer list.

Paul Cookson

Penalty I

Which side shall I put it?
Which way will he go?
Will I look a total schnook,
Or will I be a hero?

Shall I try to place it
To his left or to his right?
Or shall I try to blast it high
With all my blinkin' might?

Perhaps he'll stand up straight to it,
I can never seem to tell.
I wish I knew what he's going to do,
I don't feel very well.

I suppose I'd better take it,
I'm drowning in my sweat;
Here I go, I'll keep it low,
IT'S IN THE BACK OF THE NET!!

Penalty II

Which side will he put it?
Which way will he go?
Will I look a total schnook,
Or will I be a hero?

Will he try to place it
To my left or to my right?
Or will he try to blast it high
With all his blinkin' might?

Perhaps I should stand up to it,
I can never seem to tell.
I wish I knew what he's going to do,
I don't feel very well.

Here he comes to take it,
I'm drowning in my sweat;
Here I go, I'll just . . . Oh no!
IT'S IN THE BACK OF THE NET!!

Mike Jubb

Oath Sworn by all New Footballs

Before each match I must take a deep breath
and hold it through the game.

I must at all times be round and resilient;
able to bounce back when floored.

I must accept the odd punch
with no thoughts of revenge.

I must put up with a good kicking
without thought of retaliation.

When trapped I must be patient until released.
When cornered the player determines my escape.
At throw-ins I must be
entirely in his hands.

Though often crossed I must not be cross.

For free kicks, penalties and dead balls
I must always know my place.

I must remain modest; though I cross the line
credit goes to the striker.

While on nodding acquaintance with the players
I must at all times remain impartial.

John C. Desmond

Gabby the Groundsman

His name's Mr Gabriel, but we call him Gabby,
He wears old wellies and his tracksuit's baggy,
He rolls his own fags and makes his own wine
– And Gabby brings the oranges on at half-time.

Gabby is the groundsman down at the Rec,
He wears an old scarf round his old, skinny neck,
He puts out the corner flags and paints in the lines
– And Gabby brings the oranges on at half-time.

If ever there's a problem, he's quite prepared to ref,
(You can call him anything you like, 'cos Gabby's stone deaf)
If ever there's a problem, he'll always run the line
– And Gabby brings the oranges on at half-time.

And if you ever lose a stud, Gabby's got a spare,
He once produced a set of shirts from God knows where;
We once forgot the ball and he said, *'Ee y'are, borrow mine!'*
– And Gabby brings the oranges on at half-time.

Lots of people laugh at him, they say he's just a joke
But everyone in our team thinks he's a great bloke,
He's like an extra player, he's the joker in the pack,
He ought to have a tracksuit with his name across the back,
He's always there supporting us, rain or shine
– And Gabby brings the oranges on at half-time.

We heard it as a rumour first; we thought, *It can't be true!*
But then the rumour spread around till everybody knew
And we were really proud of him, between me and you:
We heard it in the playground, we heard it in assembly,
We saw it on the telly and it made us go all trembly:

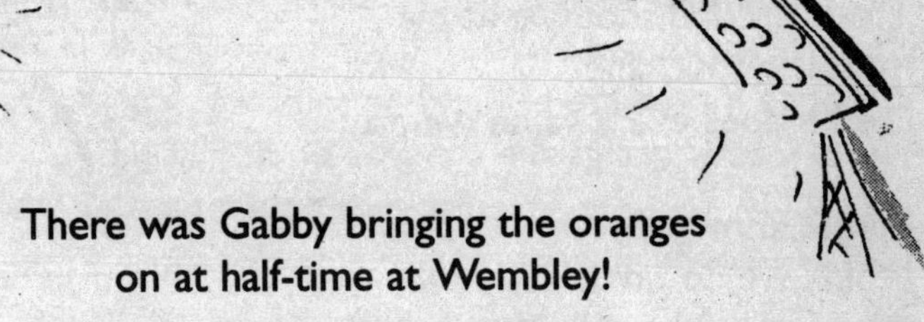

There was Gabby bringing the oranges
on at half-time at Wembley!

Tony Charles

Dazzling Derek

That's my dad shouting at me
from the touchline
like he does every game we play.

I don't know why
I think we do quite well really
this week we're only losing ten-one
and I've scored three times
twice in my goal
and once in theirs

not bad for a goalie.

Last week I was on the wing
it was brilliant
I nearly scored a million times
we still lost
but who was counting?

My dad was
he got really angry
there's no pleasing him.

What he really wants to do
is to shrink back to being ten like me
slip onto the field
score the winning goal
with seconds to go
defeat staring us in the face
Dazzling Derek saves the day!

But he can't
so he jumps up and down on the touchline
shouts at me
mutters and kicks the grass
stubs his toe and yells
nearly gets sent off the field by the ref

where's the fun in that?

David Harmer

Song of a Frustrated Scouse Winger

Over 'ere with it, Charlie!
Does it 'ave ter take a year!
On me 'ed, son, on me 'ed then,
let's 'ave it over 'ere!

Their back line's 'opeless,
goalie's a gormless clot.
Knock it over quick t' ruz,
I'll purrit in the pot!

Cum 'ed, Charlie, pass it, lad!
Are y gunna take all year?
To me left, me left foot, Charlie!
Curl it over 'ere!

D'y-raffter 'og it all yerself,
fumble it down the right,
when I am stalkin' on the left,
one big goal in sight?

A gapin' goal just dead ahead,
me properly onside
and you greedy-guts-in' with the ball,
bangin' it yards wide!

Matt Simpson

Making a Meal of It

What did you do at school today?

Played football.

Where are you going now?

To play football.

What time will you be back?

After football.

Football! Football! Football!
That's all I ever hear.

Well!

Well don't be late for tea.

OK.

We're having football casserole.

Eh?

Followed by football crumble.

What?

Washed down with a . . .

As if I can't guess!

nice pot of . . .

I'm not listening!

. . . tea.

Bernard Young

Football through the Ages

Football grew from itchy feet
kicking whatever they found in the street;
a pebble; a stick; a rolling stone;
a rusty can or an animal's bone.
The left-over bladder of a butchered pig,
inflated and tied off, was perfect to kick;
if something would roll it would do for the game
that then had not even been given a name
till, on through the ages, the game was to grow,
at long last becoming the football we know.

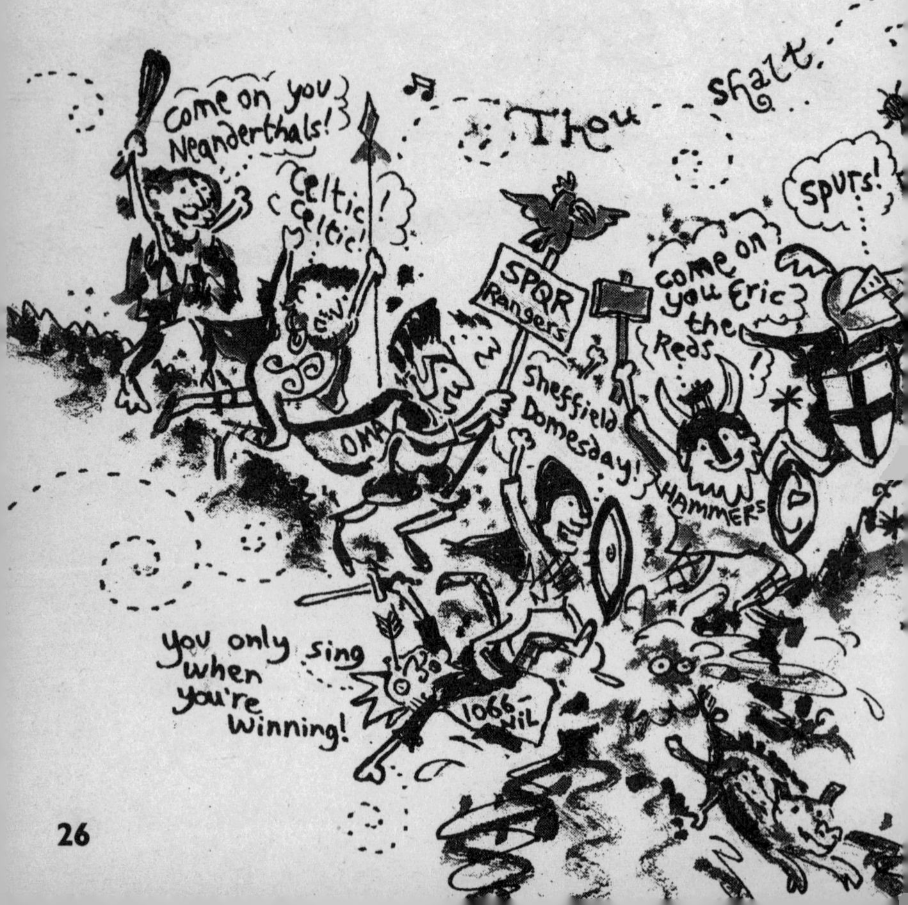

O, I'm glad of my football, I'm glad of the rules,
I'm glad of the pitches at clubs and at schools,
I'm glad of my kit, but I am even gladder
the days are long gone when they kicked a pig's bladder.

Celia Warren

Oddball

Who was it went and shifted
both sets of goalposts?
You can't see either net.
The pitch is so vast
there's no end to it, yet

the thick and nasty fog's not lifted,
there isn't a single sound.
You call and call for the ball
that's never seen or passed . . .

What's gone wrong, where are the teams?
You get an urge to take off, fast,
but with boots glued to the ground,
discover you can't move at all.

Whose are those screams?
You yell for the ref,
though the ref must be deaf:
he looks weirdly thin in that long black coat,
and then he whistles a very strange note

like nothing else you've ever heard,
before he floats off out of view.
You tell yourself you'd have preferred
staying at home – it's too cold here for you.

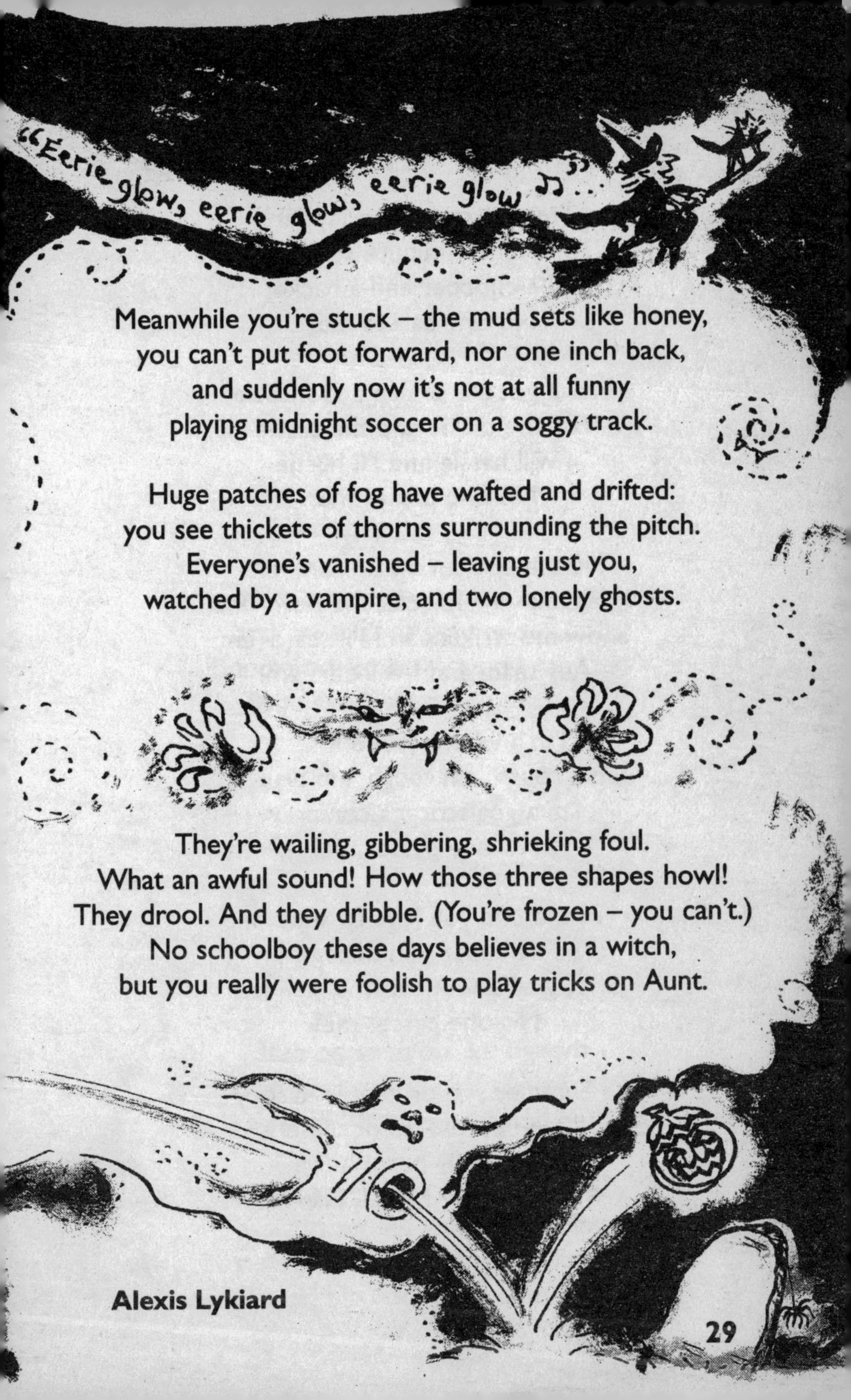

Meanwhile you're stuck – the mud sets like honey,
you can't put foot forward, nor one inch back,
and suddenly now it's not at all funny
playing midnight soccer on a soggy track.

Huge patches of fog have wafted and drifted:
you see thickets of thorns surrounding the pitch.
Everyone's vanished – leaving just you,
watched by a vampire, and two lonely ghosts.

They're wailing, gibbering, shrieking foul.
What an awful sound! How those three shapes howl!
They drool. And they dribble. (You're frozen – you can't.)
No schoolboy these days believes in a witch,
but you really were foolish to play tricks on Aunt.

Alexis Lykiard

No One Passes Me

I'm a blaster not a tapper
I'm a ninety minute scrapper
I'm a chopper and a hacker
No one passes me!

I have got the brawn and muscle
For the tackle and the tussle
I will hassle and I'll hustle
No one passes me!

Harum-scarum do or dare 'em
I will take the knocks and bear 'em
Show me strikers and I'll scare 'em
Any team and I will stir 'em!

I'm a winner not a loser
I'm a rough 'em tough 'em bruiser
I'm a goalscorer's confuser
No one passes me!

I'm the one you love to send on
The defender you depend on
Strong of sinew, tough of tendon
No one passes me!

Summer sun or winter mire
Lion-hearted do or die-er
In my belly burns a fire
I'm the one who can inspire!

I'm a last ditch tackle fighter
I'm a knee and ankle biter
Nobody will mark you tighter
No one
No one
No one
No one
No one passes me!
Right!

Paul Cookson

Hate the Rain

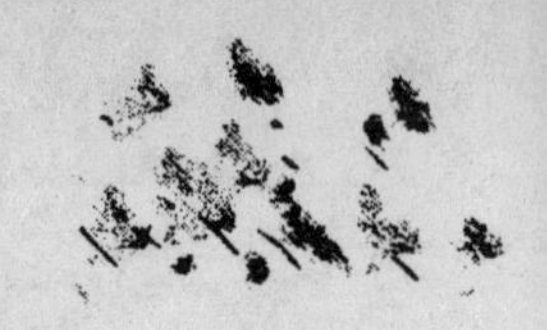

Hate the rain
Said the boy
With the mud
In his eye
Soggy boots
Chilly legs
Boggy pants.

Give me rain
In my hair
Said the boy
In the chair.
Give me mud
On my boots
And my face.

Hate the rain
Said the boy
As his shot
Skidded wide
To the laughs
And the shouts
And the chants.

Give me
One chance to play
Just five seconds
Someday
Just one kick
Just one touch
In your place.

David Clayton

HCPT

Playground Song

Footy in the playground
Red sun in the sky
I might play for England
Piggywigs might fly.

Johnny Mars picks Spanner
Johnny Mars picks Rose
Andy Platt picks Henry
Henry picks his nose.

Fifty running girls and boys
Screaming for the ball
One goal is the iron gates
One the lavvy wall.

Ghosts sit in our classroom
Ghosts climb up the stairs
Rows of ghostly children
Upright in our chairs.

Ghosts upon the school wall
Watching us each day
Crowding through the doorway
At the end of play.

Gareth Owen

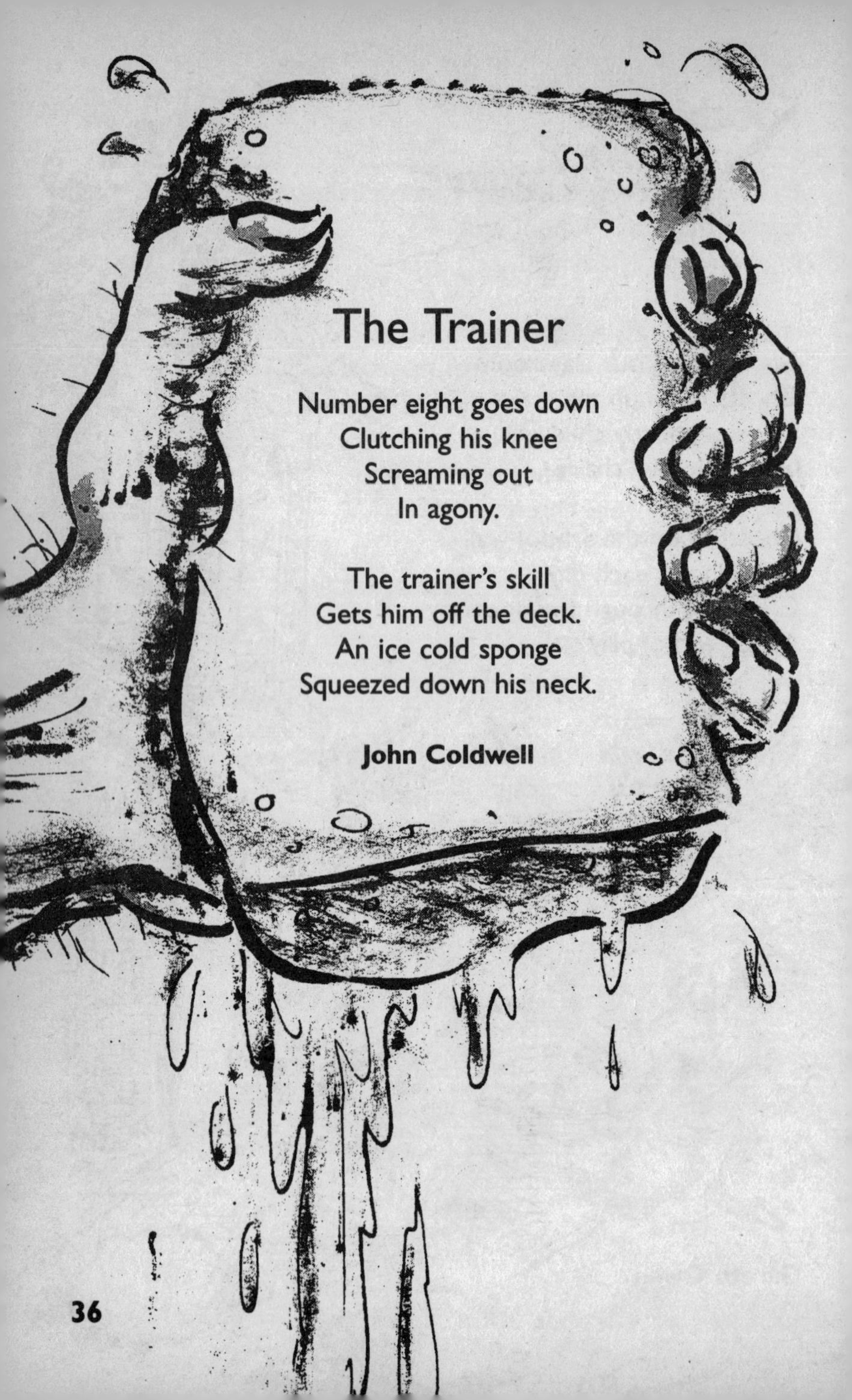

The Trainer

Number eight goes down
Clutching his knee
Screaming out
In agony.

The trainer's skill
Gets him off the deck.
An ice cold sponge
Squeezed down his neck.

John Coldwell

Footballer

By lamplight a boy is kicking a tennis ball
against the dance-school wall.
It is November but mild.

His hat is tightly wedged onto his head
and he hesitates when he sees me coming.
The street is quiet but for the ball drumming.

He makes an ungraceful angular shape
like most boys do, only his loneliness
smooths out his crooked angles.

It is as if someone long dead
had come back to life as a child
with ambitions he could not explain.

Something is wedged inside the bobble hat,
something wants to escape.
Running headlong out of dreams, the flat
realities hover about him like angels.

George Szirtes

Football Report

The Bees gave the Magpies the bird,
    And the Cherries were ripe for the picking.
The Wolves and the Lions were both on the prowl
    And the Wanderers wandered round kicking.

The Gunners were playing some big shots,
    The Blues were all down in the dumps,
The Saints were no match for the Rangers,
    But the Stamford Bridge lot came up trumps.

The Spurs gave the Hammers a battering,
    The Robins played on in the snow,
The Hornets were buzzing and stinging,
    And the Rovers knew just where to go.

The Canaries were all of a twitter,
For QPR's ground was all swampy.
The Dons' gowns kept tripping them up as they ran
And the whole crowd was roaring for Pompey.

* * * * * * * * * *

I hope you've enjoyed this short ditty!
Can't think of much else to report,
So I'm off to the other Canaries –
I've earned a suspension from sport!

Pam Gidney

RIP Offs

Here lies the body
Of your United,
Promotion hopes
Quite sadly blighted.
Meanwhile, my City's
Sitting pretty.

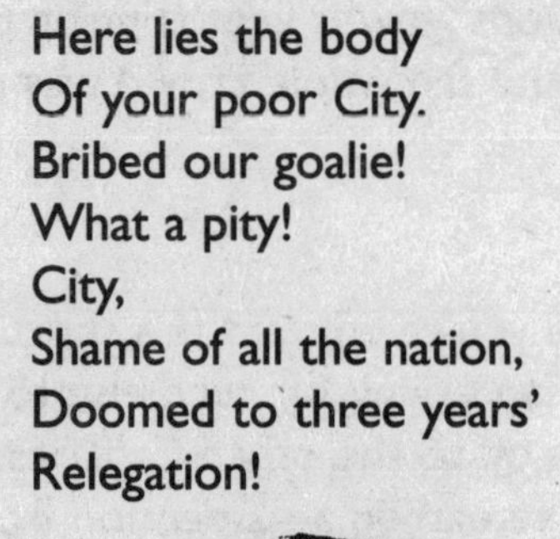

Here lies the body
Of your poor City.
Bribed our goalie!
What a pity!
City,
Shame of all the nation,
Doomed to three years'
Relegation!

Here lies the body
Of our centre back;
Beat his own goalie
With a wicked pass-back.

Here lies the body
Of a fool in the crowd:
Shouted rude words
Far too loud.

Here lies the body
Of a poor sad fan,
Faced with a life-long
Away-game ban.

Here lies the body
Of a player from City.
Got a free transfer.
What a pity!

Here lies the body
Of our first team coach,
More useless
Than an old cockroach.

Here lies the body
Of a hopeless winger.
Would have done better
As an opera singer.

Here lies the body
Of Brian Bowler,
Flattened to death
By the groundsman's roller.

Here lies the body
Of Bertie Bissell,
Swallowed the pea
In his referee's whistle.

John Kitching

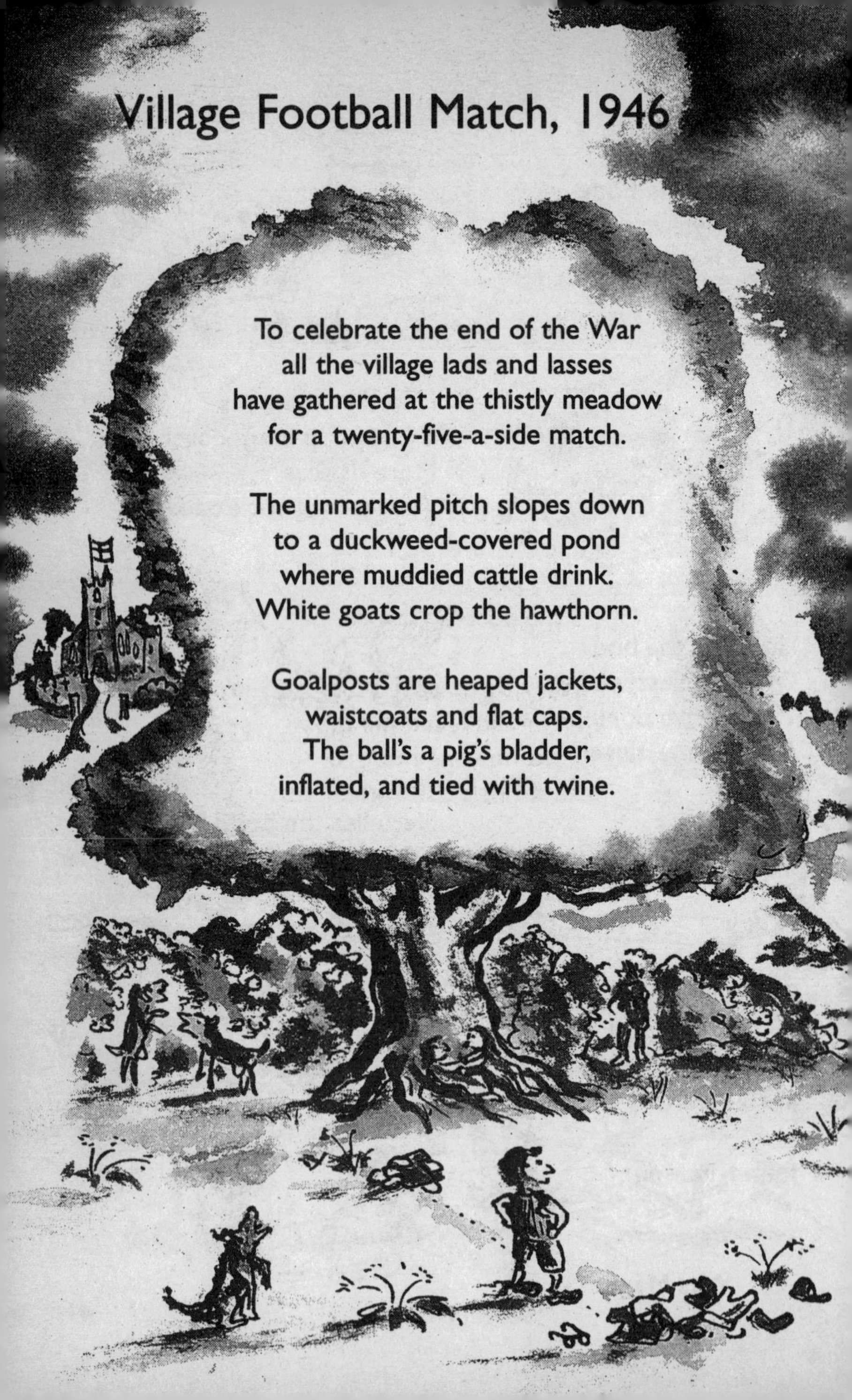

Village Football Match, 1946

To celebrate the end of the War
all the village lads and lasses
have gathered at the thistly meadow
for a twenty-five-a-side match.

The unmarked pitch slopes down
to a duckweed-covered pond
where muddied cattle drink.
White goats crop the hawthorn.

Goalposts are heaped jackets,
waistcoats and flat caps.
The ball's a pig's bladder,
inflated, and tied with twine.

Endless, the game thunders on,
on into the gloaming.
It is nineteen-all
as the purple dusk deepens.

Now only three spectators remain:
an invalid-faced full moon,
a howling mongrel
and a single astonished star.

Wes Magee

Match of the Year

I am delivered to the stadium by chauffeur-driven
limousine.
Gran and Grandpa give me a lift in their Mini.

I change into my sparkling clean world-famous designer
strip.
*I put on my brother's shorts and the T-shirt with tomato
ketchup stains.*

I give my lightweight professional boots a final shine.
I rub the mud off my trainers.

The coach gives me a final word of encouragement.
Dave, the sports master, tells me to get a move on.

I jog calmly through the tunnel out into the stadium.
I walk nervously onto the windy sports field.

The crowd roars.
Gran and Grandpa shout 'There's our Jimmy!'

The captain talks last minute tactics.
'Pass to me or I'll belt you.'

The whistle goes. The well oiled machine goes into
action.
Where did the ball go?

I pass it skilfully to our international star, Bernicci.
*I kick it away. Luckily, Big Bernard stops it before it
goes over the line.*

A free kick is awarded to the visiting Premier team. I'm
part of the impregnable defence.
*The bloke taking the kick looks six feet tall – and just
as wide . . .*

I stop the ball with a well-timed leap and head it
expertly up the field.
The ball thwacks me on the head.

The crowd shouts my name! 'Jim-meee! Jim-meee!
Jim-meee!'
Gran says, 'Eee, our Jim's fallen over.'

I don't remember any more.

Trevor Millum

Goal

There's kissing, there's shouting,
there's hugging and leaping
and swaying and singing
and a cheer from the whole
clan of supporters;
there are flags, there are banners,
there is huge celebration,
because Kenny, our hero, has scored a great goal.

O the pitch it is green with the greenness of summer,
and the roses exult, and the neighbours look over
the fence (is the cat being chased? no, thank goodness)
it is only young Kenny kicking a football
and shouting in triumph and letting the whole
neighbourhood know that he alone, Kenny,
in the back garden, sole king of the stadium,
Kenny the hero has scored a great goal.

Gerda Mayer

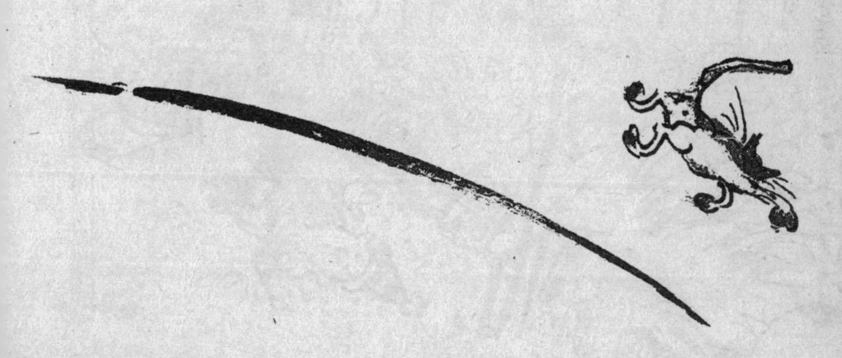

Never Put Noel in Goal

Damn! There goes another goal.
That must make it ten they stole.

Why do we suffer this terrible toll?
Because some prat put Noel in goal.

Oh, no! Not Noel.
He flaps around like a Dover sole.
We always get this rigmarole
whenever we've got Noel in goal.

So who gave Noel that role?
Who put Noel in goal?
I bet they think they're droll.

Give 'em jail with no parole.
They must be round the pole.

Noel, Noel, pathetic prole,
without one virtue to extol,
a sorry soul with no control.

Take a stroll, Noel.
Crawl back in your hole.
Quit the team, claim the dole.

A slightless mole'd
patrol our goal
better on the whole than you, Noel.

A frightened foal
could fill your role,
or a water vole
or a lump of coal.

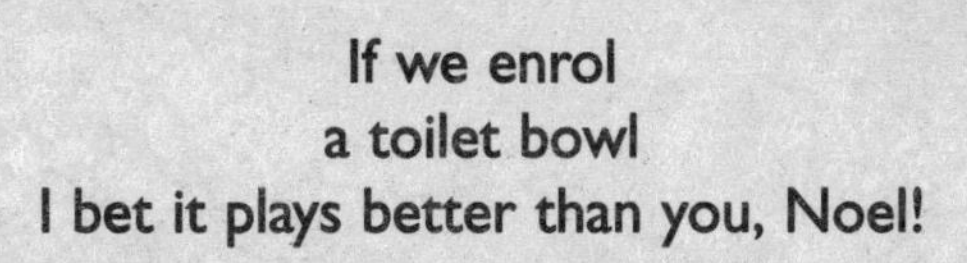

If we enrol
a toilet bowl
I bet it plays better than you, Noel!

Nick Toczek

Pantomime

HE'S BEHIND YER

shriek the red-faced fans behind the home goal.

HE'S BEHIND YER

as their red-haired keeper balances the ball on the palm of one hand.

HE'S BEHIND YER

as the red-shirted away winger jabs the ball using his head.

HE'S BEHIND YER too late as the red-raged keeper screams,

HE CAN'T DO THAT REF

OH YES HE CAN as the red-rippled net welcomes the ball.

OH NO HE CAN'T

OH YES HE CAN

OH NO HE CAN'T continues the red-carded keeper alone in the dressing room.

After the Match

Did yer see the other team?
Thee all 'ad one leg,
'ands tied behind their backs.
Ah've seen better schoolboys round our way
Kicking ball in't street.
Their kits were rubbish
Thee didn't even look the part,
More like rag and bone men.
Feller who trained 'em should ha'
Taught 'em to play football
Not nancy around with the ball
Like ballet dancers.
An' another thing.
That ref was blind
Or thee'd never ha' won.

Angela Topping

What a Team!

It's not their fancy footwork
it's not their certain skill,
it's not the way they kick the ball
that gives us such a thrill.

It's not their famous players
it's not the way they score;
it's our team's new outside loo
which makes the crowd all roar.

It's the football on the seat
to help pass the time of day,
it's the little potty underneath
for when they play away.

It's the way the toilet flushes
when someone scores a goal,
it's the name of every player
on every toilet roll.

It's the whistle on the wall
to blow when you're inside,
it's our team's new toilet
that makes their winning side.

Andrew Collett

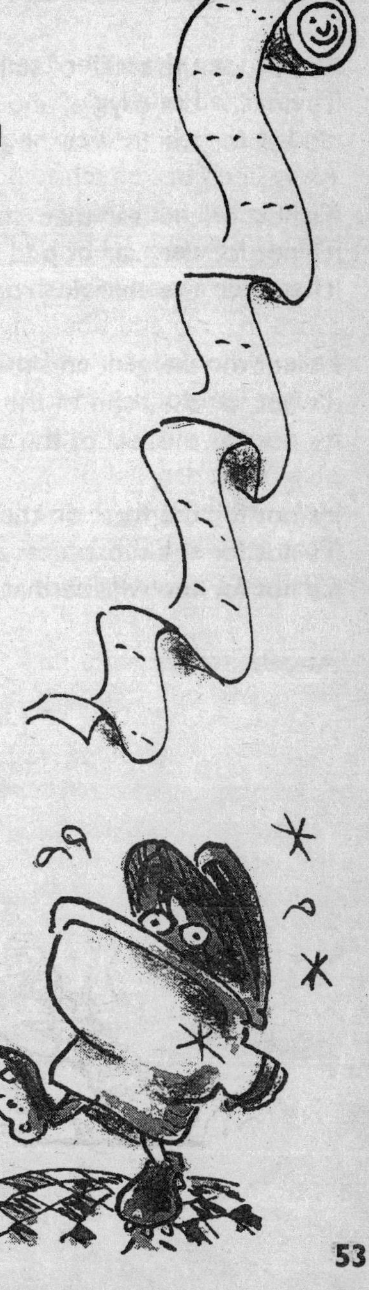

When it's all Over

It's not for the smell of stale embrocation,
It's not for the days of anticipation,
It's not for the fist-waving glad celebration;

It's not for the fear that churns up your gut,
It's not for the pair of odd socks for good luck,
It's not for the changing room door banging shut;

It's not for the glint and the gleam of the studs,
It's not for the echo of the ball's ringing thud,
It's not for the feel of the soft clinging mud;

It's not for the frost on the pitch in the morning,
It's not for the substitutes standing round yawning,
It's not for the whistle that blasts without warning;

It's not for the mist that swirls round the posts,
It's not for the other team shrouded like ghosts,
It's not for the spectators lost in their coats;

It's not for the sweat on your head when you're running,
It's not for the threat of legs bruised, grey and numbing,
It's not for the net that deceives you with cunning:

But when it's all over,
When it's all done,
Whether we've lost,
But best if we've won –
We break out the soap,
High spirits and towels,
And sing in the showers
For hours and hours.

Dave Ward

Football Facts

Things you never knew about Football

Why are there always huge, grey, furry caterpillars clinging onto television cameras?

Why does the referee make the two captains stand in the middle of the pitch in pouring rain to toss the coin when they could have done that in the nice, warm changing rooms?

Why do referees look at least eighty years old?

Why do they make the bar just that little bit too high for the goalie to reach?

Why don't the captains ever let their mascots ever play for their teams and why do they run off with the triangular pendants they swap?

Why don't they let managers sit in proper seats instead of having to hide in a trench beside the pitch?

How do substitutes always manage to get their tracksuits off without snagging their studs on the material?

Why do goalkeepers spend the entire match shouting when nobody takes a blind bit of notice?

Why do you never notice the penalty spot until there's a penalty?

Why is it that the spectators of the losing team have to leave early?

Why do all defenders have short back and sides and superstar strikers have long, curly hair?

What does the goalie need a little bag for?

If linesmen need white sticks why doesn't the FA provide them?

Gary King

So you want to be a Referee?

1. You forget your whistle at an important match. Do you:

a) cough politely each time there's a foul?
b) ask the players to own up when they commit an offence?
c) award penalties every two minutes until somebody wins?

2. A player belches and doesn't say 'Pardon'. Do you:

a) give him an indigestion sweet?
b) give him a lecture and a yellow card for being so rude?
c) make him say 'Pardon me, Referee' really loudly over the tannoy system?

3. A player coughs, spits but leaves dribble down his face. Do you:

a) give him a tissue?
b) tell him to find a tissue?
c) hand the trainer a tissue?

4. You catch the goalie making mud pies in the penalty area. Do you:

a) kick them over and flatten the pitch as best you can?
b) give him a proper bucket and spade?
c) agree they are an acceptable line of defence?

5. Two opposing players become involved in a physical tussle leading to punches being thrown. Do you:

a) pretend it hasn't happened until both sides have said sorry?
b) break it up and use your red card on them?
c) stand back and watch, give them a sharp kick in the shin when they aren't looking, then send them off?

6. A player disagrees with your decision and calls you a very rude name. Do you:

a) ask him to spell it while you write it down?
b) make him write 'I'm very sorry' 100 times?
c) call it him back with bells on?

7. It is a game at a neutral ground. Both teams play in blue and want to this time as well. Do you:

a) let them both play in blue and call it a draw?
b) toss a coin to see who changes shirts?
c) make both teams take their shirts off and paint their chests a different colour?

8. A player falls harmlessly to the ground then writhes around clutching his leg. Do you:

a) get the opposition to help him up and rub his knee better?
b) stop the game and bring on the trainer with the stretcher even though everyone knows in three minutes he'll be leaping around like a gazelle in football boots?
c) kick his other leg and send him off for time-wasting?

9. A delicate situation happens in front of you but you miss it because you're daydreaming. Do you:

a) ask the players to re-enact the situation in slow motion so that you can make the correct decision?

b) pretend there's dirt in your eye and get the linesman to sort it out?

c) ignore it and carry on the game, sending off anyone who argues?

10. It is the last five minutes of a Cup Final. The scores are level. You are hungry and want your tea. There is a dubious appeal for a penalty. Do you:

a) ignore it, uphold fair play and stay hungry?

b) go and get a pie from the pie-seller and then ignore the appeal?

c) give the penalty, finish the game early, and nip out for a double fish and chips and a greasy burger?

11. Halfway through the first half a young player lets you know that he needs the toilet.
Do you:

a) let him go back to the changing rooms?
b) tell him he should have thought of that before you started but OK, go anyway?
c) get the trainer to run on with a bucket?

12. One captain says his team have all got colds and can they wear their woolly jumpers, scarves and tracky bottoms.
Do you:

a) say yes as long as they don't get too hot and faint?
b) check they all have a note from their mums?
c) say no and make them play in their pants and vests?

If you scored mainly:

a) You softy.

b) You wishy-washy wet blanket.

c) You nasty person, you'll grow up to be a head teacher, or even a dinner lady!

Paul Cookson and David Harmer

Extra Time Quiz

Look at the drawings on pages 60 to 63.
Can you find these people in the poems earlier in the book?
Go to the top of the Premier League if you can find all of them!